All's happy
that ends
happy

D1637773

For Noak

All's happy that ends happy

Rose Lagercrantz

Eva Eriksson

GECKO PRESS

CONTENTS

Part 5

Part 6

Part 7

1

· ·

Chapter 1

It's a beautiful day in April. Easter break has just begun, and the sun is shining so brightly on Home Street that people are throwing their windows open wide.

First the ones who live in the white house, then those in the gray house, and then the people in the green house.

But in the yellow house, there's no sign of life.

No Dad comes to the door to pick up the news-paper. No Cat appears, chasing after a mouse. No girl runs out and stops to pick a crocus from the lawn, then rushes into the kitchen to put it in an eggcup.

No, there's no girl to be seen!

What girl is this? you might wonder.

Dani of course! Or Daniela, if we use her real name. But on the day we're talking about, it seems she isn't at home.

When some of her classmates turn up and ring the doorbell, no one answers it.

Cushion and Meatball and Benny want to deliver an Easter egg from the class and the teacher because Dani hasn't been to school for seven weeks. No one has seen her since before the break when she got sick.

They ring and ring the doorbell, but no one opens the door. Where is she?

"What if she's dead," says Meatball.

"In that case, it won't matter if we eat some of her egg," says Benny.

"She's not dead." Cushion keeps a firm grip on the chocolate egg. "I'll look after it until she comes home from Northbrook or wherever she is."

Benny glares. "Don't you know chocolate can go all hard and horrible," he mutters as they leave.

2

Chapter 2

But Dani wasn't in Northbrook where her best friend Ella lived.

Not even Ella was there for Easter break. She'd gone away with her mother and little sister to the island, to clean winter out of the house.

She was busy sweeping spiders' webs and dead flies from the windows and sills. Her mother could deal with the droppings under the kitchen sink.

They scrubbed and swept because soon Paddy—Ella's extra father—would be arriving at the island, and by then they wanted everything spic and span, inside and out.

As soon as they were finished indoors, her mother
Sonja hurried out to the garden to plant all the
seedlings she'd brought over from the mainland.

Ella followed her with the big, heavy watering can.

Her little sister Miranda ran off to do some
watering too with her own toy can: not the
new plants, but the dandelions growing
further away.

When Ella saw her, she put down her can and went over. "They don't need watering," she pointed out. "Dandelions are weeds. Mama doesn't like them."

"Dandelions are pretty flowers." Miranda went on watering.

Then their mother called them. It was time to go and get Paddy with the little Buster boat.

But Ella shook her head. "Miranda and I'll stay here," she called back. Then she turned to Miranda and said, "I know something fun we can do!"

"What?" Miranda asked.

"Send a message in a bottle."

"What do you mean?"

"You write a letter and put it in a bottle. Then you throw it in the sea, and it floats away to another country!"

"Why would we do that?"

"Because someone will find the bottle and read the letter!"

Ella rushed into the house to get paper, a pen and an empty bottle with a screw top.

I know exactly what to write, she said to herself. *I'll put a call out for Dani.*

Because Ella didn't know where Dani was either.

It was high time she did.

Chapter 3

Missing person ! she wrote.
I am a girl alone on an island in the archipelago.
I have only one friend in the world, but she has
gone missing. So I'm searching for her. Her name
is Dani. She is blonde, has blue eyes and is almost
always happy. But I'm not, because I'm in a stupid
class with a horrible teacher.

She stopped and waved her pen a little as if that might chase away the dark thoughts that had crept over her. Then she continued:

Dani has a father called Gianni.
And she has Sadie who lives with him.

Or, how was it now? Gianni and Sadie were engaged, but then they weren't any more! Something had gone wrong. No one knew what.

Ella chewed her pen and thought a minute.

No, that didn't have to be in the letter! The most important thing was to write about Dani so that whoever found the letter in the bottle would recognize her if they met her.

Her mother Sonja called again: "Come on, Paddy's waiting!"

But Ella shook her head. "I haven't finished my letter!"

"And I haven't finished the pretty flowers," puffed Miranda, who'd come running to fill her watering can.

"You can do that later," said their mother. "Hurry and get your life jackets."

"No, we're staying here," said Ella.
"No, you're not," said her mother.

"What if Miranda goes down to the jetty and falls in the water…"

"Then we won't have Miranda any more." Ella finished the sentence. Because that's what her mother always said when they were on the island.

"Or what if I go up to the stone pile in the forest and be bitten by a snake," added Miranda, because that's also what their mother said.

"I'll look after her," said Ella before her mother could come up with new excuses. "I won't let her out of my sight for a second."

Sonja looked at the time. "Promise me then! Not one minute!"

"Not even one second, I said!"

"Can we have ice cream if I don't go up to the stones in the forest and be bitten by the snake?" Miranda called after her.

Sonja, who was already late, just waved in reply.

Chapter 4

Miranda hurried back to the dandelions with water sloshing about in her toy can.

And Ella went back to her letter. There wasn't much room left on the paper.

This is what Dani looks like.

And if you find her,
tell her to phone me. I miss her.
I miss her day and night.
Yours sincerely,
Ella

There. Now it was ready.

She rolled up the paper, poked it into the bottle, screwed on the lid and ran over to Miranda.

"Do you want to come to the fishing cliff and watch me throw the bottle into the sea?" she asked.

Miranda shook her head.

"Why not?"

"I haven't finished watering yet."

"You've watered every flower!" said Ella.

"No, not every one," said Miranda.

"Stay here until I come back then."

Miranda nodded obediently.

"You mustn't go anywhere! Do you hear me?"

Miranda nodded again.

Ella raced off to the fishing cliff. She stood a moment to catch her breath before she threw the bottle in a wide arc over the water.

It landed with a splash and bobbed cheerfully
off on the waves.

She stayed a minute longer to watch it go.
Would anyone find it and read about her search?

Then she headed for the house.

"My Bonnie lies over the ocean, my Bonnie lies over the sea," she sang. It's a song in English that Paddy had taught her. That's how it started. And it finished: *"Bring back, bring back, oh bring back my Bonnie to me, to me."*

But now Ella changed the words a little and sang:

"My Dani is over the ocean, my Dani is over the sea. My Dani is over the ocean, oh bring back my Dani to me…"

Chapter 5

When Ella reached the house, she stopped singing and looked around.

Where was Miranda?

Not there, anyway.

"Miranda," she called.

No answer.

The empty watering can lay abandoned on the grass.

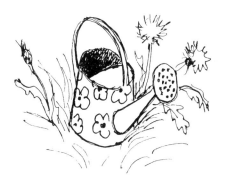

I haven't been away very long, thought Ella. A little more than a second, perhaps… But not more than a minute!

Well, maybe a little more than a minute…

"Miranda!" she called again.

No answer.

Had Miranda gone up to the stone pile on her own?

"Miraaaaanda!" yelled Ella, and she rushed up to the pile where the adder lived.

It was full of blue anemones. But there was no sign of the snake. And no sign of Miranda.

Did she go down to the jetty on her own?

No, she's probably hiding, thought Ella.

She did that sometimes to tease them, and then you had to try and find her.

"Miranda, come ouuuut!" yelled Ella. "This is not funny!"

But no matter how loud she yelled, there was no answer.

In the end she ran over to a rocky mound where you could see the jetty. But Miranda was nowhere to be seen.

Instead Ella heard a little boat approaching. Her mother was already on her way back with Paddy!

Ella was filled with panic.

What would her mother say when she found that Miranda was gone? Her mother who had always trusted Ella.

"Ella understands Miranda even better than I do," she often said.

And it was true. Like the other day in the toy shop when they were each allowed to choose a present instead of Easter chocolates.

Ella chose a necklace with turquoise beads, and Miranda wanted a beautiful big dollhouse.

"We can't buy that," said their mother. "It costs too much!"

Miranda's bottom lip started to quiver.

Their mother didn't budge. But neither did Miranda. Soon she was crying loudly.

Everyone in the shop looked at them.

"Quiet, Miranda." Their mother looked embarrassed.

Then Ella stepped in. And what did she do?

She started crying too.

She was much better at it than her little sister. She didn't howl so that people's ears hurt—no, she'd never!

Ella sobbed silently so that anyone who saw felt sorry for her.

"What's wrong with you now?" hissed their mother.

"I'm sad too!" sniffed Ella.

"Why are you sad?"

"Because my little sister can't get a dollhouse…"

Everyone listening probably thought she was the nicest big sister in the world. Anyway, that's what she thought herself.

And her mother gave in. Soon they left the shop with a new dollhouse, even though it wasn't Christmas or anyone's birthday. Just Easter.

They usually got Easter eggs, but this year it was the dollhouse and the bead necklace, and everyone was very pleased except their mother, who was now much poorer.

So, it was true that Ella could manage her little sister better than anyone else, but now that Miranda had disappeared, she didn't know what to do.

Soon her mother and Paddy would reach the jetty and wonder why the girls weren't there waiting for them.

They had no idea that one of them had disappeared. And that the other one wanted to disappear, too!

But where?

Chapter 6

Ella ran to the lookout. There she saw a big pile of branches. Paddy had put them there in the autumn, after he had felled some tall pine trees on the island.

It would be their May bonfire.

No one will look there, she thought. *I can hide in there!*

Ella crept bravely in among the branches and made herself a small cave inside the heap. It creaked and cracked when she climbed in, but she took no notice and quickly covered herself with twigs.

The dry pine needles pricked like pins and stung her skin, but her worry about what her mother would say felt a thousand times worse.

"Miranda," she whimpered. "Where have you gone? If you don't come out, I can't take another step for the rest of my life! At least, not for several weeks, anyway."

Then she turned to Dani in her mind and talked quietly to her, as they usually did when they couldn't talk to each other properly.

These thoughts worked like emergency beacons, the sort you send up from a boat that's about to be shipwrecked.

Dani, where are you? thought Ella. *You have to help me find Miranda! Hurry! Come as soon as you can.*

3

Chapter 7

But where was Dani then?

The girl who was so happy. That's what she thought, anyway. In her first year of school she wrote a book she called *My Happy Life*.

"Write more happy lives," Cushion said when the teacher read it to the class.

But she didn't get around to it at the time. And then she forgot.

Just before summer break in her second year, the teacher put a new book on Dani's desk for her to write in.

"It is high time for a sequel," she said. "*My Happy Life, Part Two,* you could call it."

Dani thought a little.

What would it be about this time?

Dani could be happy about almost anything. Sometimes she was happy just because she wasn't unhappy! Or because they were having pasta for dinner. Or noodles. Or apple pie.

She liked all food, except peas.

"They give me a cold," she said when she was small.

"You can at least try them," said Grandma.

But her father saved her.

"You don't have to eat them if you don't want to," he said.

That was when she was four.

When she was five, she was happy if she was allowed to sit in her teacher's lap at kindergarten.

When she was six, she got Cat.

Her father found her in the park when he was out running. She was lying there squeaking in a wastebasket—a little kitten who couldn't get out!

Had someone thrown her away?

They would never know.

He picked her up, put her in his hat and took her home to Dani, who was overjoyed.

When she was seven, she met Ella, and she was the happiest she'd ever been.

She stayed like that until Ella had to move away. Then she thought she would never be happy again. But she was, because she had such good classmates. Especially Cushion. She played with him all the time.

Meatball usually joined them too. And Benny.

Sometimes Vicky and Mickey got angry because she played more with the boys than with them.

But she was happiest when she could go to Northbrook and visit Ella. The annoying thing was that it took such a long time to get there, so it couldn't be often. Almost never.

Seven weeks ago, she went there alone on the train. It went well until she arrived and found that no one was there to meet her at the station.

The journey ended with her having to go all the way home again.

She didn't want to write about that in the new book.

It shouldn't be about anything except what she thought was fun. Like playing with her friends at playtime. They usually pretended to be superheroes who fought giant spiders, zombies and skeletons.

She'd been thinking of writing about that. But then she got sick.

She got tonsillitis and had to have medicine. When school started, she was still sick.

That was when things finished between Sadie and her father. Dani didn't even know why.

Dad got sad and went to visit his family in Rome to try to think about different things.

Dani could have done with that, too. She was just as sad, because that's what it's like for people who are very happy. They can become very unhappy just because they're no longer happy.

Most unhappy was Sadie. When Dani realized that, she decided to make everything right again.

But she couldn't.

The tonsillitis was followed by a terrible cough that meant Dani could hardly breathe. She coughed till she went blue in the face.

Grandpa said she must go to hospital. He didn't even wait to ring the ambulance, but wrapped her in blankets and carried her straight to the car.

Then he sped to the hospital where they x-rayed Dani's lungs.

Dani had pneumonia and she had to stay in the hospital and breathe oxygen.

Chapter 8

When Dani's father heard how sick Dani was, he came home immediately.

He sat by Dani's bed day and night, but she hardly knew he was there.

She didn't notice how often Grandma and Grandpa sat with her either.

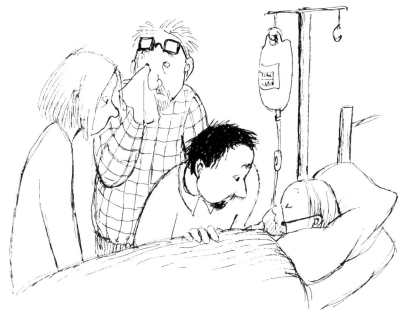

She couldn't eat or drink but was on a drip instead.
That's liquid medicine and nutrition that goes
through a needle straight into the blood.

It was a long while before she opened her eyes and discovered her father. Then she mumbled something, but no one could hear what.

Dad leaned over her. *"Amore,"* he said, "say it again!"

But Dani closed her eyes and said nothing more.

Gianni turned to Grandma and Grandpa. "Did you hear what she said?"

"Maybe she asked about her hamsters," guessed Grandpa.

"No, I thought she said Sadie!" Dad leaned over Dani again. "Do you want Sadie to come?" he asked.

Dani nodded.

"Then I'll phone her," Dad said to Grandma and Grandpa.

"Yes, do that," said Grandpa.

"Hurry up," said Grandma.

But Sadie couldn't come straight away because she'd moved to Northbrook, just like Ella. She wanted to live close to her sister Lisette who was a policewoman there.

It wasn't until the next day that Sadie stood in the doorway, looking at Dani.

Dani's father, Gianni, leapt up and offered Sadie his chair. She sank into it without looking at him.

She only had eyes for Dani, who had become so pale and thin. "Little ghost," she said. "What can I do for you?"

Then Dani said something again:

"Get married." Her voice sounded quite strange because she hadn't used it for such a long time.

Sadie gave a start and Gianni blinked in confusion.

"What did you say?" Sadie leaned forward to hear better.

"Get married," repeated Dani. "To Dad!"

"That's not possible," said Sadie. "I don't think Gianni wants to."

She glanced at Gianni.

Dani closed her eyes. They thought she had gone back to sleep, but suddenly she asked, "How can you know that?"

"He hasn't proposed to me," Sadie explained.

Dani opened her eyes again and looked at her father. "Do it then, Dad!" she hissed. "Propose to her!"

"That's not how it works, Dani-darling," said Grandpa.

"I think…I'll go and tidy up a little," Dad mumbled and got up. "I look like a ghost as well!"

It was true. Dad, who'd been sitting so long at Dani's side, was tired and unshaven. Now he took his bag and disappeared into the bathroom.

Grandma and Grandpa also got up. They said they had to go home. But it was as if they couldn't bring themselves to leave. They just stood in the doorway and moved their feet around.

Sadie began to fuss over Dani.

She helped her sit up in bed, wiped her face with a hot facecloth and combed her hair.

When Dad came out of the bathroom, he smelled of aftershave.

He turned to Sadie. "Do you think I'd make a good-enough husband?" he asked.

It didn't sound like much of a proposal. He should have rehearsed it first, thought Dani.

Sadie didn't answer.

"Can't we go and have a cup of coffee?" asked Dad.

"NO, stay here!" squeaked Dani.

"We'll only be away for a moment," Dad promised.

"And we'll stay for a little longer," said Grandpa. Grandma nodded.

When Gianni and Sadie came back, they looked very solemn. Sadie looked as if she'd been crying.

"Didn't he propose?" asked Dani, disappointed.

"Propose?"

Sadie turned to Gianni. "Did you propose?"

"I thought I did…" said Dad.

"The parking meter has run out," Grandpa interrupted, and he rushed off with Grandma.

"Propose one more time," said Dani.

Dad turned to Sadie. "Love can be so difficult…" he began.

Wrong again, thought Dani. He should have started with something else.

But Sadie didn't think so. "Love is better than no love," she said, and she hugged him. "I love you as you are."

A big smile spread over Dani's face, one that hadn't been seen there for a long time.

When Dad and Sadie thought she'd gone back to sleep, they began to talk quietly to each other.

But Dani was only pretending. She lay listening to every word they said.

In the end she couldn't keep quiet any longer.

"Didn't I tell you I'd make everything right?" she asked.

They looked at her in surprise.

"You said that?" said Sadie.

"Yeah…"

"I don't remember."

"Then maybe I just thought it," Dani mumbled.

She didn't have the energy to say everything she thought, because then she'd do nothing but talk.

That's how it had always been. And still was. She thought non-stop—almost, at least.

Soon she fell properly asleep.

Chapter 9

During the days that followed, Dani thought a lot about what would happen now. Would there be a wedding?

She knew all about weddings. She'd seen them on TV. Whenever a princess was having a wedding her grandma would call her and they'd sit on the sofa and hold hands while they watched.

That was how Dani imagined it would be when Dad and Sadie got married:

First two flower girls would skip in, sprinkling rose petals along the church aisle.

One of the flower girls, whose name would be Daniela, would toss white rose petals. The other, called Ella, would scatter red ones.

They would have wreaths of roses in their hair—white and red—and their dresses would look as if they were made of roses.

Everything would be roses!

And the whole church would be full of people, sitting and waiting in the pews.

Grandma and Grandpa.

And cousin Sven and his mother.

And Ella's mother and little sister and extra father Paddy.

And all of Dani's class with the teacher, sitting in a group.

And then we mustn't forget Sadie's sister, Lisette, she thought. Lisette has to come too! In her police uniform.

All the people who Dani knew and loved would be sitting there, waiting to see the bride and bridegroom.

Tam, ta ta ta! would suddenly thunder from the big organ.

Dani painted the scene for herself, over and over. The bride and groom up by the altar! And the priest who said: "Now I ask you, Sadie Maria Gustafsson, do you take Giovanni Valentino Ziliotto to be your lawful wedded husband, in sickness and in health?"

And Sadie would have to say yes!

Then the priest would ask if Gianni would take Sadie.

Dad couldn't say the wrong thing then!

Everything would be so beautiful, Dani thought. The bride, the bridegroom, the music. And the flower girls. Especially the flower girls!

"As long as I haven't dreamt the whole thing," she sighed anxiously.

Chapter 10

But when Dani came home from the hospital, she found that she hadn't dreamed up anything. Dad and Sadie were really getting married. But not in a church.

Dani thought she hadn't heard properly.

She shot up in the sofa where she had been lying and resting.

"But where are we supposed to scatter the rose petals?" she asked.

Dad didn't understand.

"But you'll have flower girls at least?"

"No, no flower girls," said Dad. "Sadie and I are getting married at the Swedish embassy in Rome."

Dani didn't know what the Swedish embassy in Rome was, but she soon learned. It is a house where they look after Swedish things, in Italy.

"If a Swede is robbed, they can go to the embassy and borrow money to get home again," Dad explained. "And if anyone wants to get married there, that's also fine."

Dani looked at him in surprise.

"It will just be a small wedding," he carried on. "I've already been married once. With your mother. Having a big new wedding would feel like letting her down. It will just be me and Sadie…"

When he saw Dani's face, he realized. "Yes, and you too, of course!"

"And Ella," Dani pointed out.

"Ella?"

"We have to scatter rose petals at that Swedish thing, whatever it's called."

"It's called the embassy," said Dad. "No, there won't be any rose petals. No big event, I said. Just a little family gathering. And Ella is out of the question!"

"Then I'm also out of the question," said Dani.

Dad's face grew dark, and Dani tried to control herself.

She had to watch out, because now Dad was finally happy. It was important that he didn't get sad again.

But Ella mustn't be sad either, and she would be if she heard that she wasn't invited to the wedding. It was probably best to keep quiet about it. How could Dani manage that?

The safest thing would be to not talk to Ella at all, she thought. Not until the wedding was over.

"Can Grandma and Grandpa come then?" she asked, snuggling closer to Dad.

He hesitated.

"They're the ones who look after me when you're sad," Dani reminded him. "So, they should be with us when you're happy as well!"

Dad gave in.

But it turned out that it was only Grandma who wanted to come. Grandpa preferred to stay home and look after Cat and the hamsters. And go to the jazz festival with his old friends.

After some thinking, Dad said that Sadie's sister Lisette should also come. She could come the day before the wedding, along with the bride.

"Then that's enough!" he said, putting a finger in the air.

4

Chapter 11

So that was how Dani went to Rome at the start of the Easter break, even though she was still coughing.

But the worst thing was that she couldn't get over Ella having to stay at home.

Not even the sight of all her relatives waiting for them at Arrivals put her in a better mood.

There were Granny Lucia and Granny's sister Antonella waving their arms.

And Gianni's brother Giuseppe with his wife Donatella and their children Roseanna and Alessandro.

Even Gianni's cousin Mario had come to welcome them.

They all wanted to kiss and hug Dani before they took her away to Mario's car. He was the one taking them home…

…to Granny Lucia's little apartment in the middle of town.

But how would Dani and her dad and grandma fit into it?

It was so hot and cramped, it was hard to breathe. Luckily there was a balcony!

Dani opened the balcony door and stepped out to get some air, but immediately Granny Lucia pulled her back in.

"She's scared you'll fall off!" Dad explained.

"I don't fall off balconies!" said Dani. "I'm not a toddler!"

"While we're here, we'll do things Granny's way." Dad closed the door.

"Where shall we all sleep?" Grandma asked.

There was only one bed and that was Granny Lucia's.

Grandma had to take the sofa. Dani had a mattress on the floor. And Dad would spend the night with cousin Mario, who lived in the same building.

Mario was a pianist and in his little apartment there was only room for a big black grand piano. Dad would sleep underneath it.

Mario himself would sleep in the wardrobe with the door open to make room for his legs.

"Don't worry about how we'll sleep," said Dad to Grandma and Dani, "because we won't be here very much. Granny Lucia is going to show us around town."

Grandma thought that was a good idea. She wanted to go out at once and admire all the sights.

Soon they were walking through many narrow streets. Dani held tight to Dad's hand, so she wouldn't get lost in the crowd.

The whole time Granny Lucia kept stopping to point out things she wanted them to look at.

They weren't allowed to rest until they reached the Roman Forum, where the old Romans had their meetings one or two thousand years ago.

But now there were only ruins left.

"If you haven't visited them, you haven't been to Rome," said Granny Lucia.

That was the first day.

Chapter 12

The second day in Rome was almost the same,
except that Granny's sister Antonella came to show
them things and
point and talk
in Italian.

They walked and walked…

…until they came to the Vatican where the pope lives.

They stood in a long line to go in and see the lovely paintings on the ceiling.

Granny Lucia's sister Antonella said that if you haven't seen the paintings, you haven't been in Rome.

Inside, everyone walked around, looking up. Dani too, until she felt dizzy and had to look down.

She wasn't so interested in old ceiling paintings. But she would have been if Ella was there.

She tried not to think about Ella, but she did anyway.

In the end she could think of nothing else.

Granny Lucia and Antonella noticed that something was wrong.

"Is Daniela sad?" they asked. In Italian.

Dad translated.

Dani nodded, but Dad shook his head.

"Look at the angels!" he said. "Aren't they beautiful?"

Dani didn't answer.

"She's a little tired," Dad explained to them. "She's been sick."

"She might be hungry as well," Granny Lucia pointed out, and she took some Italian bread from her handbag.

The bread was rock hard. Dani pretended to chew it but hid it in her pocket as soon as everyone looked up at the ceiling again.

She would have really liked a good bun, preferably the type Grandma made, but Granny Lucia wasn't like Dani's grandma.

She didn't care about baking or cooking. She was only interested in people.

"She talks on the phone for eight hours a day," said Dad. "Usually with her sister Antonella. As soon as they're apart, they phone one another.

"They've had so much fun since they became widows and Antonella moved to the same street as Lucia. And best of all is showing their extraordinary city to people who visit."

When they came to the famous Spanish steps, Dani couldn't look any more. She sat down on a step to rest.

She would rather have been with her cousins, but they didn't have Easter break yet, so she had to be with the grown-ups who just walked and walked. And talked and talked. In Italian.

Until her ears hurt.

The worst was when they came to the Colosseum.

"That's a colossal arena where slaves in the olden days were forced to fight wild animals," Granny Lucia explained.

Dad translated.

"Haven't you been to Rome if you haven't seen the Colosseum?" asked Dani.

"No, you probably haven't," said Dad.

But Dani didn't like stories about people who were forced to fight wild animals. She got scared hearing about all the terrible things that used to happen in the world. Still happened, actually.

"I don't want to be here," she said. "Won't Sadie come soon? I've come here to go to a wedding."

"I have too, come to think of it," Dad said. "It must be time to go and see if Sadie and Lisette have landed."

The rest of the day, Granny Lucia and her sister had to show their beautiful city only to Grandma, who went eagerly along with them. She wanted to be able to tell her bridge friends that she had really been in Rome.

But Dad went off in a taxi with Dani to see if Sadie had landed.

She had. Sadie was in Rome now too, waiting in a café with her sister.

Chapter 13

It was a loving reunion. Dani and Dad both
brightened up and started talking about everything
between heaven and earth. In Swedish.

"Can I have a gelato?" Dani asked, patting her father on the arm. That's the word for ice cream in Italian.

"Of course," said Dad. "There's a fantastic ice cream bar around the corner!"

"Come on then!" Dani pulled him by the arm.

"Sure," said Dad, and carried on talking.

Dani decided to go a little ahead and see what sorts of gelato they had.

She went to the street out in front and looked around all the corners without finding the fantastic ice cream bar. Just a fantastic fountain in the middle of a big square. And in front of it, a fantastic dog stretched out like a black lion. She had to have a closer look.

Because that's how it was in Dani's life—dogs always appeared when she was least expecting them.

This one lay completely still, waiting for the man who seemed to be his owner to stop talking on his phone.

Dani went up to them. "What's the dog's name?" she asked.

The man, who seemed to understand her Swedish, interrupted his conversation and said, "Nero."

"Hi Nero," said Dani, and she got a beautiful look in return.

She stroked the dog's shiny fur and he wagged his tail.

Nero's owner passed her the leash and made a sweeping gesture with his hand.

He seemed to be suggesting she walk around the square with the dog.

Maybe he could tell by looking at Dani that she was good with animals?

Dani was pleased and Nero gave an enthusiastic bark. He knew exactly where they wanted to go, and he went off with Dani in tow.

She could only follow.

Dani pulled on the leash to calm him down, but Nero just went faster.

"Stop!" said Dani, but of course Nero only understood Italian, and it was impossible to stop him.

When he suddenly turned into a side street, Dani put down her feet and pulled on the leash as hard as she could. With no result. Where was he going?

At last he came to a stop and lifted his leg against a building.

Dani took the chance to catch her breath.

As soon as Nero had
finished, he carried on
down another street.
And then down a third.

He didn't stop until they
came to a door where
someone had put out a
big bowl of water.

He drank it in a single go.

Slurp slurp slurp, was the sound.

He must have been very thirsty.

Then he lay down in front of the door and refused to move.

"Come on!" Dani told him. "We have to go back. Your owner will be worried if we're away too long."

But the dog stayed where he was. It wasn't until Nero's owner came puffing and opened the door that he got up and slunk inside.

"Grazie, bambina." The man held out a bright red treat wrapped in cellophane.

It looked tempting, but Dani shook her head. "I'm not allowed to accept things from people I don't know," she said.

The man kept pressing it on her, until she remembered no in Italian. *"No!"* she said, clearly.

"Arrivederci," he replied in a hurt voice. That means goodbye.

He went in and let the door close behind him.

Chapter 14

Dani looked around. Now she had to hurry back to the cafe. But where had she come from?

She quickly went back and turned the corner, but she didn't recognize anything. She had just hung onto the dog without noticing where they were going.

Dad's probably wondering where I am, she thought. I hope he doesn't think I've been... What was it called again?

She couldn't get the word out.

She went even faster and turned another corner and arrived at a square, but not the one with the big fountain.

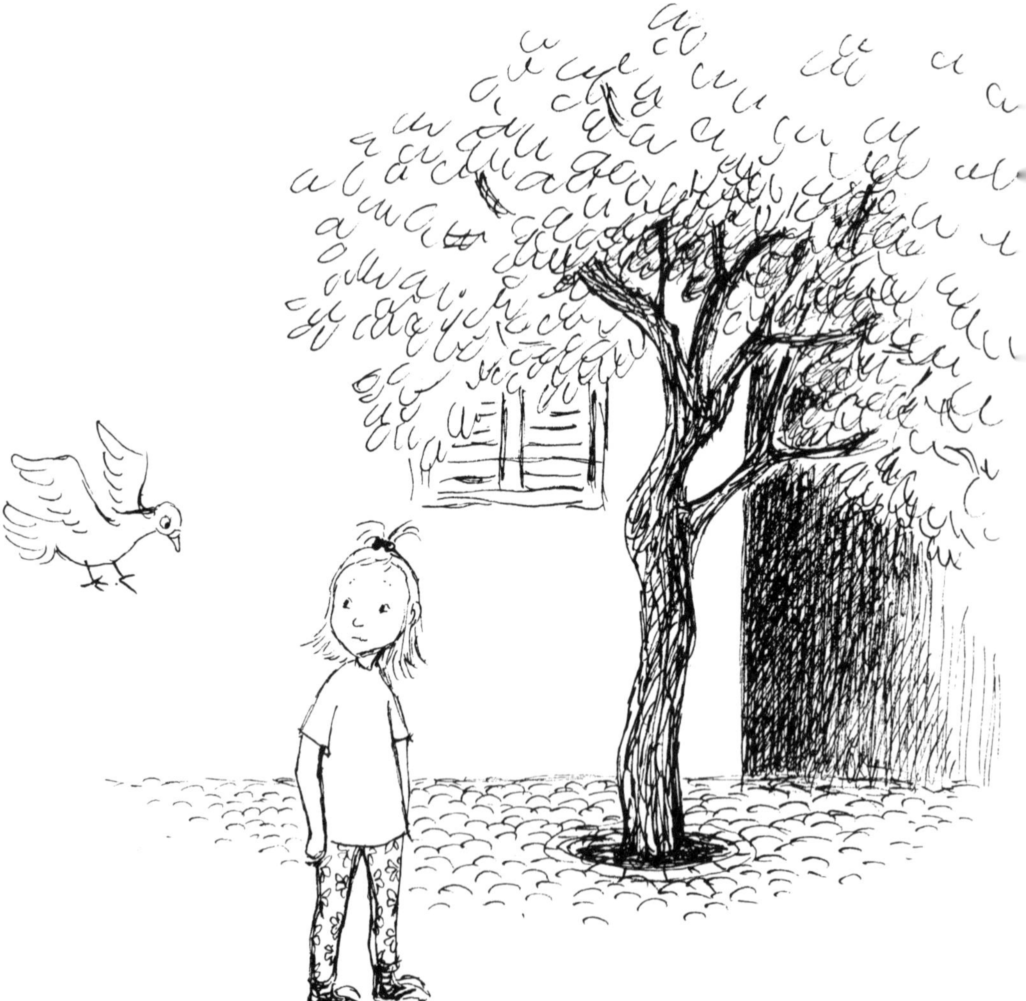

The square was small and shabby and completely empty. The only living thing she could see was a white pigeon, which flew over and landed at her feet.

"Little bird," she said. "Are you all alone too?"

Then she remembered Granny Lucia's bread, and she fished it from her pocket.

"Come on, little bird, come here, there's something for you."

She broke the bread into pieces and let some of them fall to the ground. The pigeon pecked at one immediately.

Suddenly a whole flock of pigeons appeared out of nowhere and started to quarrel over the bread.

Dani had to chase them away so the little white one could eat in peace.

But they came back!

Dani threw them the other half of the bread and let them fight over it.

When they had pecked it all up, they disappeared, the little white one too. And Dani was on her own again.

Now she had to work out how to find her way back
to Dad. She'd been busy feeding the birds instead of
thinking about that!

She started to feel very uneasy.

"This isn't really true," she said to herself.

That's what she often told herself when something
bad happened in the books Grandma read to her.
Then she'd put a finger to Grandma's lips. That
meant she'd had enough.

This wasn't happening in a book, though. It was in
real life. Dani was lost in Rome and there was no
one she could ask the way.

In the drab little square, it was so quiet and still she
could hear her own thoughts.

Ella, she heard herself think. *I don't want to be
here any more.*

She heard it loud and clear, as if she'd actually
said it.

Then she heard something else, a big voice
shouting:

"DANI!"

And Dad came rushing towards her!

"DAD!" she yelled and threw her arms around him.

He lifted her up and hugged her hard…

...before putting her down with a thump.

"What are you doing here?"

Yes, what was she doing here?

"I was looking for the fantastic ice cream bar," she remembered. "But then I met a dog..."

"Bah!" said Dad. "You're not a little kid who has to dash after every dog you see!"

"I didn't dash! The man gave me the leash."

"What man?"

"The dog's owner! He let me look after it, but Nero was thirsty and had to run home for a drink!"

"Dani, this can't be true," Dad sighed. "And the dog's owner let you go off on your own?"

"He was nice! He gave me a treat!"

"He gave you treats?"

"Yes, but I didn't take it. You've told me I mustn't take anything from strangers."

Nothing Dani said was any use. Dad was in a bad mood again. It was only when Dani got a coughing attack that he composed himself, gave her a throat lozenge and took her hand.

"Come on, let's hurry back to Sadie. She's beside herself with worry."

Chapter 15

When they arrived at the café it got even worse.

Lisette scolded her: "Don't you know what could have happened?"

"What?"

Dani could feel tears coming.

"Don't start crying now," said Lisette. "You have to understand that you can't go off on your own in a city like Rome!"

"We're not angry with you," said Sadie. "We just got so scared. We didn't know what had happened. You could have been kidnapped!"

Dani took a breath. That was it, the word she had been looking for! Kidnapped!

"I don't think you should blame someone who's almost been kidnapped," she sniffed.

Sadie softened. "Come on," she said to Dani. "You and I can go for a little walk to calm ourselves down."

And when Dad wanted to come too, Sadie shook her head.

"You wait here."

She took Dani's hand and off they went.

"What is really the matter?" she asked, handing over a handkerchief.

"I don't want to be here!" Dani explained.

"Why not? Have you forgotten we have a wedding in the morning?"

Dani shook her head.

"And then we're going to Venice, you, me and Dad!"

"Are we?"

"Yes, but it's a surprise," said Sadie.

Dani swallowed.

"Do I have to come?" she asked.

"Yes, you do!"

"Why?"

"Because I have something special to tell you when we get there," said Sadie.

But Dani stopped and wouldn't budge. "I won't come to Venice. I don't want to be there either."

"Where do you want to be, then?"

"With Ella."

Sadie turned away and looked in a shop window.

"Look!" she said suddenly. "Look at the beautiful things they have in this shop."

She pointed to a little baby top with a big red heart on its front.

In the middle of the heart it said:

TI AMO

"That means, 'I love you,'" Sadie translated.

"I know that," Dani giggled. "Dad says it all the time."

"Maybe you'd like a little present from here?" Sadie suggested.

"Do you mean something for Ella?"

Sadie opened the door and went in without answering. Dani followed.

Chapter 16

A bell rang crisply and the shopkeeper smiled at them.

Dani looked around. The shop was filled from floor to ceiling with fun things. On a table were beautiful animal masks.

She picked up a cat mask and held to her face.

"Miaow," she said.

But Sadie didn't seem to be listening. She held up a baby top like the one in the window.

"Isn't this sweet?"

"Mmm." Dani slid the cat mask to one side. "But I don't play with dolls any more. Only cuddly toys."

"This isn't for a doll, it's for a real baby," said Sadie.

But now it was Dani who wasn't listening. She put the mask back on her face and purred.

"Miaow!"

The shopkeeper started to laugh.

"You can have that. And I'll take the baby top," said Sadie.

"What about Ella?"

Sadie was busy paying and didn't hear her. And Dani didn't dare ask again.

Sadie shouldn't get in a bad mood, now she was getting married and everything.

"Do you play with dolls?" Dani asked in surprise as they had left the shop.

"I told you, it's not for a doll."

"Who's it for then?"

"I'll tell you when we get to Venice."

But Dani didn't accept that. "I want to know now!"

Sadie took a big breath: "Your little sister. You're going to be a big sister."

Dani stared at her through the holes in the mask.

"Does Dad know about this?" she asked finally.

"No, he doesn't know a thing. Promise not to tell him! I want to do it myself."

Dani closed her eyes. It was as if a small sun had lit up inside her.

"Do you hear me, Dani? Do you promise not to say anything?"

"What will she be called?"

"What do you think?"

"Sun," said Dani.

"Sun?" Sadie was surprised. "But what if she's a grumpy baby?"

"No," Dani smiled. "My little sister won't be a grumpy baby!"

Chapter 17

Dad was sitting in the café waiting.

Lisette had gone to the hairdresser to get her hair done, and he didn't understand what Sadie and Dani were up to.

"Was it necessary to buy that right now?" he said when they appeared with the cat mask.

"Yes, it was," said Sadie. "It's important that everyone is happy when we get married. Especially Dani!"

"And Ella," said Dani.

"That's enough!" Dad warned. "Not another word about Ella!"

"But Gianni!" said Sadie.

"Dani never seems to realize that she'll get other new friends," Dad complained.

"But not another best friend," muttered Dani, looking ready to burst into tears. The sun that lit up her insides had gone into cloud.

Sadie looked crossly at Gianni.

"You're the one who doesn't realize," she told him. "That's not what this is about!"

"So what is it about?"

"Faithfulness," Sadie explained. "Dani can't forget her first friendship. She's like you. You couldn't forget your first love! It was only when I broke off our engagement that you understood that I meant something to you too!"

Sadie had become red in the face and she turned away.

"Do we have to argue about that again?" Gianni was annoyed. "The day before we get married!"

"Think about me, then: remember I was the one who came and made everything right!" Dani reminded them.

"Yes, you did!" Sadie agreed. "Sorry. I think I'm a little tired after the journey. I'll go to the hotel for a rest. And Gianni, make sure Dani gets something to eat!"

"Spaghetti," said Dani, patting her stomach.

"Dani, you're not sad any more?" Dad asked when Sadie was gone.

"No, I'm happy!" Dani remembered. "But I'm not allowed to say why."

"Can't you?"

Dani pulled on the mask and purred. Suddenly Dad started to laugh.

"That's fun, that cat mask," he agreed.

"Do you think?"

Dad nodded.

"Shall we go back to the shop and buy one the same for Ella? Would you like that?"

Dani's mouth fell open. Sometimes she didn't understand her father.

One minute she wasn't allowed to say a word about Ella, and then he suggested they go and buy a present for her.

"That's exactly what I want." She nodded happily.

"Then we'll go and eat spaghetti and then we'll go home to Granny Lucia and relax," said Dad.

That night Dani went to bed early.

She was so tired that Grandma didn't even need to read her a goodnight story.

Grandma, who had sore feet from walking around the whole day with Granny Lucia and her sister Antonella, had a foot bath instead.

5

Chapter 18

The first thing Dani thought of when she woke up the next morning was what she wasn't allowed to tell.

"Did I say anything in the night?" she asked, sitting up on her mattress.

"You laughed," said Grandma.

"Did I? I must have dreamed about Sun!"

She bit her lip.

But Grandma thought Dani was talking about the weather.

"I agree, it would be a shame if it rained," she said, looking out the window.

"But it looks like a lovely day."

Then there was only time for eating breakfast and having a shower and washing hair. And then putting on the new dress that Granny Lucia had bought her —not a rose dress, unfortunately, but a yellow silk dress with small pearls sewn on.

And Granny Lucia's sister Antonella arrived with tights made from white lace and lots of glittering hairclips. But the best of all were the shoes, real shoes with heels. The first she'd ever had.

Dani was decorated like never before.

Then it was time to go to the embassy. It was time for Gianni to have a new wife and for Sadie to have a husband!

And for Dani to get a nice extra mother!

The ceremony went quickly. Both said yes.

Dani held the bridal bouquet while Gianni put the ring on Sadie's finger.

Sadie wasn't wearing a princess crown, just a flower in her hair, but she was still as beautiful as a princess, Dani thought.

But if Gianni thought they'd just have a simple lunch afterwards, he thought wrong.

When they came out onto the street, lots of people were waiting for them.

The news had spread that Gianni was getting married again, and now relatives and friends had gathered from near and far to congratulate the bridal pair.

A happy crowd accompanied them to Granny Lucia's.

There, in her courtyard, Gianni's brother Giuseppe and his wife had set up lots of tables and chairs…

…and set the tables with tablecloths and all the plates, knives, forks and glasses they could find.

And someone had hung up long rows of bright lanterns.

In Grandma's little kitchen a cook was squashed in with two helpers making lunch. It smelled wonderful.

Beautiful music flowed out through a window. It was cousin Mario playing his piano.

Food was being cooked in his kitchen, too, and the kitchen boys ran back and forth between the kitchen and the courtyard.

All the guests were dressed up and happy.

And everyone cheered and shouted: "Long live the bride and groom!"

Chapter 19

There were eleven courses for lunch. Dani only managed the first one, which was pasta and truffle sauce.

It was so good that she ate up everything on her plate except the sauce. She put that to one side.

Gianni made toasts and speeches, in Swedish and Italian. All jumbled together.

He talked about the first time he met Sadie. It was after he got run over and ended up in hospital.

When he woke up, he thought he was seeing an angel. That was the nurse, Sadie.

Everyone listened carefully. Dani took Grandma's
hand and squeezed it hard and Grandma squeezed back.

Even Lisette seemed moved. Unfortunately, she
wasn't wearing her police uniform but a lime green
outfit instead. It was nice, though.

But the best part was when Dani at last got to meet all her cousins and relatives and lots of other children.

Soon she ran off with them to play.

They were all there, even Dani's special cousin Roseanna, even though she had become a teenager since last time.

When they played hide and seek Roseanna
thought they should all hide in the kitchen where
Roberto the kitchen boy was busy decorating
the wedding cake. But it wasn't a good place.

As soon as Roseanna saw Roberto, she
started flirting with him! And Roberto got all
flustered, because he had to finish the cake.

Soon it was time to go back to the tables because now all the guests would sing and play.

And how they sang! Dani had never heard anything like it. Even little Alessandro sounded like an opera singer, although he was no older than Dani.

Lisette also sang for the bridal couple. A Swedish folk song that Sadie liked: "I will pick wood violets and bind them in a crown…" she sang with her deep voice.

It was so beautiful that Dani shivered.

In the end it was Gianni's turn. He chose a love song by Mozart.

And Sadie shone!

Chapter 20

And so it went on for hours, with food and talk and music. And games that were fun for everyone.

When it began to get dark the lanterns were lit, and Granny Lucia went around and lit all the candles on the tables.

Now it was time for the magnificent cake.

Sadie cut the first piece and passed it to Dani.

It was good! But it would have been even better if Ella was there too. Ella would have loved the cake!

Dani hadn't thought of her once in the whole day. She'd been having so much fun.

But now she pushed her plate away.

"You don't want any more?" Grandma asked.

"No," said Dani, snuggling into her.

Grandma was the only one at the party who didn't look really happy. Maybe she was remembering when Gianni had married her daughter, who became Dani's mother.

"Are you thinking of my mother?" Dani asked.

"Yes, I am," said Grandma.

"Was she a beautiful bride too?"

"Yes, very beautiful," Grandma said.

"It's a shame I wasn't born so I could have seen her!"

Grandma agreed, and Dani patted her soft cheek. "Can I ask you something else?"

"Of course you can, dearest heart," said Grandma.

"Are you going home again tomorrow?"

"Yes, I am," said Grandma. "It will be nice to go home to Grandpa."

"Can I come with you?"

Grandma was a little surprised—and cautious.

"You're welcome to come," she said, "as long as Gianni and Sadie are fine with that."

"Can you go and talk to them, Grandma?"

"I don't think that's a good idea, when they're about to dance the bridal waltz."

"Then I'll do it myself," said Dani, getting up.

She went and found Sadie, who was busy trying to clean a coffee stain from her dress.

Lisette was helping her.

"Sadie, does it matter if I don't come to Venice tomorrow?" asked Dani.

"Yes, it does!" said Sadie. "Don't you remember what's going to happen there?"

"Yeeee-s."

"What's that?" Lisette wanted to know.

"Sadie's going to tell—"

"Quiet, Dani!"

"I want to go home," said Dani. "Can't you talk to Dad?"

"No, I can't," said Sadie.

Dani sighed and made her way to Gianni, who was talking to some musicians in the dance band.

"Dad," she said. "I have to ask you something."

"What's that, *Amore*?"

"You mustn't be sad!"

"Why would I be? I've had enough of sad, as Sadie and I say."

"Good," said Dani. *"Molto bene!"*

It was a little bit of Italian. Very good, it meant.

Dad smiled in surprise and Dani got ready.

"Can I go home with Grandma tomorrow?"

For a moment it looked as if it would go well.

The corners of Dad's mouth were still up.

But then they went down.

When Sadie came to get him for the waltz, he
was complaining loudly.

"I've arranged a wonderful trip to Venice for us, and now Dani is here saying—"

"I don't need to come with you," Dani interrupted. "I already know what's going to happen there."

"What's that?"

Sadie gave her a warning glance, but Dani didn't notice.

"Sadie's going to tell you that I'm going to be a big sister..."

Sadie turned away and Dani stopped abruptly.

Had Dad heard what she said?

Yes, he had. He gave a happy yelp and threw himself at Sadie.

"Is it true?" he cried.

Then Dani took the opportunity to ask once more:

"Can I? Can I go home with Grandma? Answer, Dad!"

The moment couldn't have been better. Gianni was completely overcome with the big news.

"Do whatever you like!" he shouted to Dani and lifted Sadie in his arms. "Sadie, darling, when will it be?"

The answer was drowned in music, because now the dance band was tuning up.

Dad put Sadie down again and bowed to her: "May I?"

They danced away in front of all the people and Dani ran back to Grandma.

"I can!" she puffed.

"Good!" said Grandma. "Then I don't need to travel on my own! Did Dad say that he'd book your ticket?"

"No," said Dani. "We can do that ourselves."

"And do you think we can manage that?"

"Yes, we can. We can do everything, Grandma! I know where my ticket is."

When the dancing was under way and the guests were swinging around the dance floor, Dani and Grandma sneaked off to Granny Lucia's apartment to phone the airline.

After a lot of trouble on the telephone, Grandma cried in triumph: "We did it! It's all arranged. The plane goes at ten past nine tomorrow morning."

"And then I'll go to Ella's," smiled Dani. "I'm on my way, Ella."

Chapter 21

The next day Dani and Grandma woke early and got themselves ready. They couldn't get away quick enough.

Dani was afraid that Dad would change his mind, and Grandma was afraid that they would miss the plane.

Just as they were about to leave, Dad and Sadie's voices were heard on the stairs.

The bridal pair, who had stayed at a hotel for their wedding night, had come to say a drowsy farewell.

Right after that, Dad's cousin Mario burst through the door. He also wanted to say goodbye to Dani and Grandma, and he couldn't stop talking, even though the taxi was waiting.

At the same time, Granny Lucia's sister Antonella appeared with a present for Grandma: a cushion with small kittens on it that she'd embroidered herself.

These last-minute farewells meant that they were late to the airport.

Grandma was desperate and Dani was so upset she had a coughing fit.

But it turned out that the plane was late too. Relieved, they sat down with the other passengers and waited.

Grandma took a crossword from her bag and told Dani to look for her schoolwork in her backpack. She was very worried that Dani had got behind in her schoolwork, since she'd been away for so long.

But how could Dani concentrate on schoolwork? She could think only of how it would be to see her best friend again at last.

And Mama Sonja! And Paddy! And Miranda, who could say such funny things.

"Shall we catch the kiss?" Miranda once said.

She didn't know the difference between bus and kiss!

Dani laughed to herself.

But suddenly she became serious.

"What do you think Ella will say when she hears that Dad and Sadie have got married?"

Grandma looked up from the crossword. "She'll think that's fun."

"Even though she wasn't invited to the wedding?"

"Don't worry!" said Grandma. "Ella will be so pleased to see you she'll forget about everything else."

"Have you talked to Sonja?"

"Yes, I have. I talked to her last night when you'd gone to sleep and asked if you could come to them for Easter."

"And can I?"

"Sonja said it was the best thing possible! They're on the island."

Everything seemed to be turning out as Dani had planned.

First, she'd go home with Grandma and talk a little with Grandpa and rest for a day.

Then Grandpa would drive her to Northbrook, where Paddy would be waiting for her with his car.

"But I want to be a surprise for Ella."

"No problem," said Grandma. "Sonja knows that. Now if you can't concentrate on your schoolwork, you can take out the new diary the teacher gave you."

Dani hunted in the backpack.

There it was, her unwritten happy life, part two.

Grandma handed her a pencil and an eraser.

But Dani found it hard to gather her thoughts.

She couldn't write a thing until she knew for sure that Ella forgave her for not being invited to the wedding.

And apart from that, she couldn't anyway because it was time to board the plane.

STOCKHOLM ARN
BOARDING

6

Chapter 22

And now the moment was near when Dani and Ella would meet again.

It happened to be the same day that Ella sent the letter in a bottle and lost her little sister. And Ella hid herself in the pile of branches that was going to be a bonfire.

She was crouched among the prickly branches so she wouldn't have to say that her little sister had disappeared.

She thought her mother had gone to the mainland to get Paddy. She had no idea that Sonja was collecting Dani as well.

From her hiding place she could only see
branches, but she heard the boat land at the jetty.

Then she heard Paddy's happy voice calling:

"Ella! Miranda! Come and look! We have a
surprise for you!"

But she sat perfectly still without making a noise.
Not until an ant bit her big toe. Then she had to
whimper a little, because it hurt.

It couldn't be heard from the jetty where Dani was standing and looking around.

From her point of view everything had gone better than expected. The long journey was over, and at last Dani had reached Ella's. But she was nowhere to be seen.

Where was she?

Dani turned her head this way and that, like a little owl.

While Paddy and Sonja unloaded the boat she just stood there, looking. She was afraid that the worst had happened and that Ella was angry with her because she wasn't invited to the wedding.

When Sonja and Paddy left the jetty and carried the luggage up the cliff, Dani followed. The whole time she was looking for Ella.

There was no Ella to be seen.

Finally she had to ask: "Sonja, where is Ella?"

"I've no idea." Sonja was also puzzled.

"She doesn't know that Dani's come," Paddy reminded them. "We didn't say anything. That's how you wanted it, Dani."

"Yes, I did," said Dani.

So that's how it was the day Dani and Ella would finally meet again.

One of them sitting in a pile of branches on the lookout mound, not daring to put her nose out for fear of what had happened to her little sister.

And the other one afraid that her best friend would be so disappointed that she wouldn't want to see her ever again.

Chapter 23

Luckily Dani had a suitcase full of presents for Ella, enough for a whole present trail.

The case was the one Dani had prepared seven weeks before, when she went alone on the train to surprise Ella on her birthday and no one came to the station to fetch her.

And Dani had to go home again with all her presents.

She never unpacked the suitcase because she got sick on the journey home.

Then once she was home, she got even sicker and ended up in hospital. But now she'd brought it again.

"Run off and look for Ella," said Paddy when they reached the house.

"Not yet! First I have to lay out the present trail," Dani explained.

Paddy knew what she meant. He was the one who taught them a long time ago how to do a present trail. You have to hide the parcels here and there. And you give a word or two as a clue to the person who'll do the looking.

For example: "Mermaid stone."

That was a special stone where they played mermaids.

Or: "Ostrich."

That was a pine tree that had grown to look like an ostrich.

Or: "Fern garden."

"Hurry up then!" said Paddy. "If Ella has a present trail it'll be a double surprise."

Dani ran into the house to put down her backpack before going off with the suitcase to hide the first parcel.

She'd got to know every place on the island the previous summer when she was with Ella for almost the whole break. She'd climbed all the trees you could climb and swum in almost every bay.

She'd even been up on the stone heap at the edge of the forest where you don't go because snakes live there.

She began with the mermaid stone, which stuck out a little bit into the water. That was the most beautiful place, so the best present could go there.

She took off her socks and shoes and rolled up her trousers. Then she stood on the beach and hesitated. Then she said, "I don't care how cold it is; I'll just get in."

Bravely she went into the water.

The cold was terrible! Ideally she would have shrieked, but she managed not to.

With her teeth clenched she waded out to the mermaid stone and put the parcel on it…

…before tiptoeing back to the beach and putting on her socks and shoes.

Her feet felt like ice blocks!

But she had to keep on going. Ella might turn up any moment and it would be best if the present trail was all ready.

She kept going as fast as she could with the suitcase and didn't see Ella anywhere.

She didn't see Miranda either. Where could they be?

Chapter 24

Soon all the presents were nicely placed around the island, except for one. Dani couldn't find a good place for it.

Not until she came across the lookout mound with a tower of branches on it. It wasn't there last summer.

She could hide the last parcel there, she thought, and headed towards it.

She squatted down and hid the parcel between a couple of branches.

"This one won't be so easy to find," she murmured happily.

The next moment she pulled her hand back. Something was moving in there amongst the branches!

A snake?

No, it was bigger! A fox?

She bent down again and looked in, ready to run away quick as a flash.

Then she saw something!

"Ella!" she shrieked. "What are you doing in there?"

"Quiet," whispered Ella.

"Come out!"

"I can't!"

"Are you stuck?"

"No, but…"

Ella wriggled out of her hiding place.

What a mess she looked!

Her face was scratched and her hair and clothes were covered in needles and bits of tree.

"What are you doing?" Dani asked.

Ella glared. "Go away!" she said.

"W…w...why?" stammered Dani.

But she didn't need to ask. She knew the answer. Ella didn't want to see her any more because Dani was the friend who had let her down.

With burning cheeks, Dani left the lookout.

Her legs hardly obeyed her. When she'd gone a little way she turned.

"I understand that you can't forgive me, but I'm saying sorry anyway," she called.

Ella didn't seem to care.

And Dani understood. Really. What was a present trail compared to a wedding in Rome?

She trudged away until the old cough came back and rattled her.

"Anyhow, I've laid out a present trail for you,"
she managed to say between coughs.

Chapter 25

When Dani returned to the house, she had another coughing fit.

Paddy was on his way outside with a coffee tray. He stopped on the steps and gave her a worried look.

"How are you?"

Dani held up the last parcel, which was so small it fit in the palm of her hand.

"I have one parcel left, but I don't know where to put it."

"Come on, I'll help you." Paddy put down the tray.

They went together into the house, and Paddy crept to the bedroom door.

"Here," he whispered.

Why was everyone whispering all the time?
Dani threw the present onto the bedroom floor.

"No, no," Paddy whispered. "Not there! Ella will see it straight away! She has to search a little bit first!"

He picked up the little package and placed it under the bed so it could hardly be seen, then he closed the door quietly behind them.

"Now you can go and get Ella," he said. "I don't know where she is. Why hasn't she come to say hello?"

Chapter 26

Dani trudged back to the pile of branches, but she
didn't have to go the whole way.

Ella had left the
lookout and was
waiting for her behind
a pine tree.

"Where does the present
trail begin?" she asked.

What? Did Ella want
her presents after all?

It seemed so.

"Give me a clue," she commanded, sounding almost like normal.

Was it possible that she'd forgiven Dani? A present trail could work miracles!

Dani got excited.

"The mermaid stone," she called.

"Shh!" Ella hissed. "They'll hear us!"

"The mermaid stone," Dani repeated quietly.

"But it's in the water! How did you get to it?"

"I waded out! I said: I don't care how cold it is! I'll just get in."

Ella laughed.

"Come on!" she said and galloped off.

And Dani followed her.

When they went past the kitchen window, Ella slowed down and crouched low.

"Why are you doing that?" asked Dani.

"Shh! So they won't see us!"

It must be a new game, Dani thought, and she
hurried after her towards the beach.

But when they reached the mermaid stone, the present was no longer there. It had blown off and was bobbing on the waves.

Quickly Ella did what Dani had done a while ago. She pulled off her socks and shoes and rolled up her trousers.

"I don't care how cold it is, I'll just go in!" she said, rushing into the water, gasping at the cold.

She hurried over and rescued the parcel before it disappeared behind the jumble of boulders they'd named Pirate's Castle last summer.

Back on the beach she ripped it open and saw: the ring with the blue stone that Dani's mother had when she was little.

She turned it around and held it up to the light, before putting it on her finger.

"Beautiful," she admitted.

But was she pleased with it?

Hard to say.

"Next clue!" Ella ordered.

"Ostrich."

Ella knew exactly what Dani meant.

Behind the ostrich was the parcel with the rubber
duck.

Ella usually thinks rubber ducks are fun,
but now she just said: "Next clue!"

"The fern garden."

In the middle of the tangle of tall ferns was the parcel with the fan that Dani's grandma had bought when she was in Spain.

Ella said nothing about that either. She didn't seem to be pleased with anything.

"Next!"

"The secret mushroom place."

Ella rushed to the secret mushroom place with Dani coughing along behind her.

She soon found the parcel with the book about the girl who was sold to a circus.

But Ella had already read it.

Soon they'd found all the presents in the trail except for the last one, and they went back to the house.

Outside, Sonja had put out three glasses with warm blackcurrant cordial: a glass for Dani, one for Ella, and one for…

"Where's Miranda?" asked Dani.

At that moment Paddy came out.

"So, there you are," he said when he saw Ella. "Here I am with the best surprise—Dani in person! And a present trail as well! But what do I get? Not even a hug!"

Ella pretended not to hear him.

Paddy took her chin and made her look at him.

"Do you hear me, Ella, what's the matter?"

Ella turned away.

"Are you a grumpster today?"

Dani hurried over and stood behind Ella. "No, she's not," she said, "but we aren't finished with the present trail yet. We've got the last parcel still to go."

Paddy muttered something but let Ella go.

"Clue?" asked Ella.

Dani pointed into the house.

"Bedroom."

Chapter 27

Ella rushed inside and Dani followed close behind, but not all the way.

"I'll wait here," she said, stopping in the kitchen.

She knew that the last parcel wasn't much to celebrate: a seven-week-old jam cake!

Dani stood and waited for Ella to make the sorrowful discovery, when she heard Ella cry out with joy.

Dani rushed to the bedroom, where Ella was dancing around as if she'd gone crazy.

"Thank you, Dani! Thanks for coming to rescue me!"

Dani didn't understand at all.

Then Dani saw Miranda peeping out from her
mother Sonja's duvet. She blinked at them happily.

"Miranda! Oh, my little Miranda Panda!"
Ella sang.

Then she stopped and turned to Dani: "How come you hid her here?"

Dani still didn't understand a thing.

Miranda had got so tired from watering all the dandelions that she went and lay down in her mother's bed and fell asleep.

That was while Ella was over at the fishing cliff throwing her bottle into the sea.

But Ella thought that Dani had found Miranda somewhere and wrapped her in her mother's quilt, as a present among all the other presents.

"I knew it!" she squealed. "I knew it!"

"Knew what?"

"That everything would be all right, if only you'd come." Ella added: "You've saved my life!"

Dani was still puzzled, but what did it matter now that Ella was back in a good mood?

It was only when Sonja came to remind them that the cordial was getting cold that they left the bedroom.

"They didn't have any ice cream at the kiosk yet," she said, "but maybe this will do just as well."

She took four bars of chocolate from her jacket pocket.

"Here you are! One for Dani!"

"Thank you," said Dani.

"One for Ella!"

"Thank you…"

"And two for Miranda!" said Miranda, taking the other bars of chocolate.

"That's not fair!" Ella protested.

"Not fair for you," said Miranda. "But fair for me!"

And she'd get away with it this time.

Paddy, who should have had the fourth, had no chocolate. But he didn't mind, he said. As long as Ella was happy again.

"Are you?" he asked.

"Yes, I am, you can see I am," answered Ella. "Don't nag!"

Chapter 28

But with Ella you could never be completely sure. Her moods were like the weather just then: April weather. Dani knew that. Rain one moment and sun the next. And you didn't know what it depended on.

Had Ella really forgiven her?

A little later, when they stood up on the fishing cliff and looked out to sea, Dani found the courage to ask: "Aren't you angry with me any more?"

"Angry? Why should I be?" Ella wondered.

"Because you didn't get invited to the wedding."

"What wedding?"

"Dad and Sadie's."

"Did they get married?"

Ella turned to look in surprise at Dani, who was still prepared for the worst.

But the worst didn't happen. Ella just turned back again and went on staring out over the sea.

"What are you looking at?" Dani asked in the end.

"I'm looking for a letter in a bottle. I sent one today and now I'm waiting for an answer."

"Letters in bottles can take a very long time," Dani pointed out. "Several years."

"I know," Ella sighed. "But in the end a bottle will turn up. Or someone might come rowing from another island."

"Who would that be?"

"Someone who read my letter and feels as lonely as I do."

"Do you feel lonely, Ella?"

"Yes, sometimes."

"When, then?"

"When I lose Miranda."

Dani looked at her in surprise. "Have you ever done that?"

"It has happened…" mumbled Ella. "Can we talk about something else now?"

"Or play," suggested Dani. "Build a hut?"

Ella thought that was a good idea.

They went and got tools and a few planks that Paddy had lying in a shed.

But they'd hardly begun nailing when Ella put down her hammer.

"Did you forget about me at the wedding?" she asked.

"Yes," Dani admitted quietly. "But only during the day. As soon as it was evening, I remembered you."

"When exactly?"

"When I tasted the cake."

"Was it good?"

"Yes, but it would have tasted better if you'd been with me. When I thought that you couldn't taste it, I couldn't eat any."

"Okay, now let's play something!"

"What, do you think?"

"We can pretend we're two poor children with nowhere to live and we have to build a house before the storm comes!" Ella started hammering again.

Soon they were busy hammering and nailing, until Paddy called that it was time to go in and eat.

Only then did they take a rest.

Chapter 29

At the dinner table Sonja wanted to hear what the wedding was like.

"Good," said Dani. "But it would have been better if Ella was there."

Ella nodded appreciatively.

"And what was Rome like?" asked Paddy.

"Good," said Dani.

"But it would have been better if I was there," added Ella.

"Is it true what your grandma said, that you wanted to come here rather than go to Venice?" asked Sonja.

"Much more," said Dani.

"Did anything else happen in Italy?" asked Paddy.

"Well, I almost got kidnapped," Dani remembered.

"Gosh, how awful," cried Sonja.

"How did that happen?" Paddy asked.

"An old man wanted to give me a treat!"

"But dear child!" cried Sonja. "What happened then?"

"I didn't take it."

"That's good," Ella nodded. "I wouldn't have either."

Then Dani remembered something else: "I'm going to be a big sister!"

"Fancy keeping quiet about that until now!" Sonja exclaimed.

"Yes, I had to. I promised Sadie not to say anything."

"But now you've said it anyway!" Ella laughed, sounding like an old hen. "Can we leave the table?"

They ran off to sort out some presents for Miranda. She'd have her own present trail.

They took her blow-up ball, which hardly had any air in it, a baby doll and a few other small things and wrapped everything in paper.

"It doesn't matter if Miranda only gets her old things," Ella explained. "My little sister will be happy just to have parcels."

Dani saw this with her own eyes when they went with Miranda and helped her to look.

She was especially pleased when she unwrapped White Lamb, the little cuddly lamb she slept with every night.

When she found White Lamb she was beside herself with excitement.

Chapter 30

But how was Ella?

Was she really happy again?

"Tell me," asked Dani when they'd gone to bed that night. "Are you sure you aren't sad because you couldn't come to the wedding?"

"A little," Ella admitted. "But I forgive you. As long as you don't forget me again!"

"I swear on my ponytail." Dani put her hand to her head. "As long as I don't lose my memory!"

"Yes, of course…"

They lay silent for a short while.

"I forgot something important," Dani
remembered.

"What's that?"

"The best present. Go and stand in front of the
mirror and close your eyes!"

Ella hopped out of bed and ran over to the mirror
while Dani rummaged in her backpack.

"Now shut your eyes!"

She had the cat masks. She put one on Ella's face
and the other on herself.

Ella opened her eyes and laughed happily.

"Exactly what I've been wanting!"

"It was Dad who bought it," said Dani.

"Prrrrr." Ella sounded like a real cat. "What a
nice father you have."

"I know," Dani admitted.

That night Ella slept with the cat mask on her face.
Soon she was snuffling as peacefully as her little
sister Miranda in the bed alongside.

But Dani rummaged in the backpack again until she
found her diary and pen.
   At last she was ready for *My Happy Life, Part Two*.

This book is about my best friend Ella, **she began.**

She forgives me for anything.

Even when she wasn't invited to my father's wedding!

I love her and she loves me, but we don't know how

our story will end.

We are so small still.

Maybe we won't know each other when we are grown up?

But now, when we are small, we love each other.

Love is better than no love.

She stopped: where did those words come from?

She was too tired to think about it.

She closed the book and snuggled down into bed, pulling the duvet up to her chin.

Soon Sonja came and turned the light out.

"Thank you, Dani, for coming and making everything right," she whispered in the dark.

"Mmm," Dani whispered back. "Didn't I say that? It's my speciality."

"No, you didn't say so," Sonja smiled, "but it shows anyway."

"I don't have time to say everything," sighed Dani. "There's such a lot happening, you see."

"I do see," replied Sonja.

But Dani didn't hear her; she was already falling asleep.

7

Chapter 31

But what about Cushion, someone might be wondering.

How was he at the end of this day?

Unusually good, in fact.

That evening when he was taking his dog for a walk, he met his teacher.

"Hello Cushion," she said. "I have good news! Dani is well again and will be back at school after Easter break. You've still got her Easter egg?"

Cushion lit up.

"I've only tasted a little bit to make sure it's still fresh."

"And is it?"

"Yeah…"

"Good! Then you don't need to taste any more," said the teacher. "Otherwise there'll be none left for Dani."

She smiled and went on her way. And Cushion went his. He thought about seeing Dani again soon and, without knowing, he started to whistle.

It's the sort of thing he's good at.

Cushion is good at most things. He never lets the ball into the goal. As soon as the ball comes, he throws himself at it into the mud, no hesitation.

If you weighed all the mud he's had on him since he became goalie, it would weigh at least as much as an elephant.

But he's best at stopping arguments in the school yard.

"Call for the airbag," someone cries, when there's a fight in the air.

And he's there in an instant. If the fighters want to attack him, he just says: "Stop! I'm a man of peace."

Chapter 32

And if anyone's wondering what happened to Ella's letter in a bottle, it ended up a few sea miles north of the island.

It was found by an old man fishing in his dinghy.

He picked it up with his cap, unscrewed the lid and took out the letter. But he'd left his glasses at home and couldn't read what was on the paper, so he put it in the bottle again and threw it back into the sea.

With a small splash, it fell in the water and carried on its journey with the waves.

One day it might be found by someone who reads what it says in the letter—that Ella is putting out a call for her best friend in the world, Dani.

But now that you've read this book, you know that Dani has been found and that everything is fine and happy, at least for now.

Have you read the other books about Dani?

Dani is probably the happiest person she knows. She's happy because she's going to start school. She's been waiting to go to school her whole life. Then things get even better—she meets Ella.

This is a story about Dani, who's always happy. She's unhappy too, now and then, but she doesn't count those times. But she does miss her friend Ella, who moved to another town.

It's the second-to-last day of school and Dani's so happy she could write a book about it! In fact, that's exactly what she's done. But then she gets some bad news. How will she ever be happy again?

It's Dani's first summer break—her best one ever! Dani is staying on an island with Ella. They play all day long. They build huts, fish and spy on wild animals. They go swimming five, six, seven times a day.

Dani is on a school trip to the zoo when she gets lost. Then she sees someone she recognizes: Ella! Dani has to choose whether to follow her best friend in the world or follow the teacher's instructions.

Dani's father is away and Dani is staying with her grandparents. When she remembers it's Ella's birthday, she thinks of the world's best gift for the world's best friend: she, Dani, will be the present! The only thing is, she'll have to go there on her own.

This edition first published in 2020 by Gecko Press
PO Box 9335, Marion Square, Wellington 6141, New Zealand
info@geckopress.com

English-language edition © Gecko Press Ltd 2020

First published by Bonnier Carlsen, Stockholm, Sweden
Published in the English language by arrangement
with Bonnier Rights, Stockholm, Sweden
Original title: *Kärlek är bättre än ingen kärlek*
Text © Rose Lagercrantz 2019
Illustrations © Eva Eriksson 2019

Translated by Julia Marshall
Edited by Penelope Todd
Typesetting by Vida & Luke Kelly
Printed in China by Everbest Printing Co. Ltd,
an accredited ISO 14001 & FSC-certified printer

Hardback (USA): 978-1-776572-92-2
Paperback ISBN: 978-1-776572-93-9
Ebook available

For more curiously good books, visit geckopress.com